The Sphere
of Septimus

SIMON ROSE

The Sphere of Septimus

VANCOUVER   LONDON

Text © 2014 by Simon Rose
Cover illustration © 2014 by Kim La Fave
Map © 2014 Shed Simas
Cover design by Elisa Gutiérrez
Book design by Jacqueline Wang

Released in the USA and the UK in 2015

Mixed Sources

Cert no. SW-COC-001271
© 1996 FSC

FSC

Inside pages printed on FSC certified paper using vegetable-based inks.

Printed in Canada by Sunrise Printing, Vancouver, BC

2 4 6 8 10 9 7 5 3 1

Cataloguing-in-Publication Data for this book
is available from The British Library.

Library and Archives Canada Cataloguing in Publication

Rose, Simon, 1961-, author
The sphere of Septimus / Simon Rose.

ISBN 978-1-896580-75-3 (bound)

I. Title.

PS8585.O7335S64 2014   jC813'.6   C2014-904501-8

*This book is dedicated to my father and to
the enduring power of childhood memories
to inspire the imagination.*

— S.R.

*The publisher wishes to thank
Dierdre Salisbury, Ria Nishikawara and Alice Fleerackers
for their editorial help with the book.*

*Tradewind Books thanks the Governments of Canada and
British Columbia for the financial support they have extended
through the Canada Book Fund, Livres Canada Books, the Canada
Council for the Arts, the British Columbia Arts Council and
the British Columbia Book Publishing Tax Credit program.*

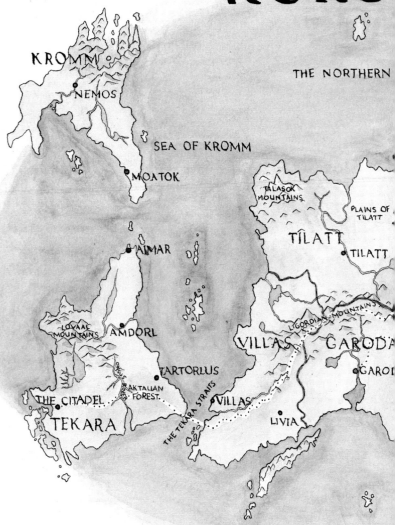

KORO

KROMM

NEMOS

THE NORTHERN

SEA OF KROMM

MOATOK

TALASOK
MOUNTAINS

PLAINS OF
TILATT

TÎLATT

TILATT

ALMAR

LOVAAL
MOUNTAINS
AMDORL

LIGORDIAN MOUNTAINS

VILLAS

GARODA

TARTORLUS

GAROD

THE CITADEL

AKTALIAN
FOREST

VILLAS

TEKARA

THE TEKARA STRAITS

LIVIA

CONTENTS

CHAPTER ONE

SEPTIMUS SEVERUS TRINKET

THE train stopped at the station. The sun was shining brightly, and Eric was relieved to see that it had stopped raining. He picked up his bag and followed the other passengers off. Everyone greeted loved ones and walked toward waiting cars and taxis, but there was no one there to meet Eric. So he put in his earphones to listen to some music and leaned against a wall to wait.

The train station emptied, except for a woman working at the kiosk and a man sweeping the floor.

Suddenly someone rushed in and bumped into Eric.

"Hey!" Eric snapped. "Watch where you're going!"

"Oh my! I do apologize," said the man. "Most sincerely, I'm so sorry. It's just that I had to dash over here. Family business, don't you know, most inconvenient. I was only recently informed I was to meet my son Eric and . . ."

The man looked down at Eric. "Why, it must be you!" He reached out and shook his hand energetically. "I'm your father, Septimus."

Eric barely recognized him. "Oh—hi, Dad."

"How perfectly splendid, most agreeable. Forgive me for not recognizing you. My, how you've grown!"

Eric hadn't seen his father in eight years, not since he was five years old. Septimus was in his late forties. He had a thick greying beard, which desperately needed trimming, and was wearing an old-fashioned motorcycle helmet. Goggles rested on his forehead. He was wearing a drab grey blazer, which was missing several buttons and had leather patches sewn over the elbows. Dangling from his blazer pocket was a gold watch chain, and bright-red socks peeked out from beneath the legs of his dark-green trousers. His shoes were scuffed and obviously hadn't been cleaned for a long time.

"Septimus Severus Trinket, at your service," he said with a broad smile and a quick bow. Then he took out his pocket watch, glanced at the time, and stuffed it back into his blazer pocket. "Well, best be off, I suppose." He picked up Eric's bag. "We can't stand around here all day, can we?"

Septimus led Eric to a battered old motorcycle with a rusty sidecar. He pulled a collection of keys from his pocket and gestured to Eric to hop in. "Don't worry about Toby."

"Toby?"

"Toby," Septimus echoed. A black sheepdog with a small patch of white hair on its chest was sprawled across the seat. It stared at Eric. "Don't fret, he won't bite. There should be just enough room for both of you."

"Are you sure?"

"Certainly," Septimus replied.

Eric reluctantly hoisted himself into the seat, slipping in behind the dog, who growled menacingly, as he squeezed onto the floor of the sidecar.

"Hold on to your bag," Septimus said, lifting it onto Eric's lap. "And put this on." He handed Eric a crash helmet and kick-started the motorcycle. The engine roared to life.

Eric was thrown back into his seat as they pulled away.

They whisked past a medieval church topped by a tall twisted spire. The busy streets soon gave way to the twisting lanes of the Derbyshire countryside. Cows and sheep grazed contentedly in green fields bordered by stone walls and hedgerows. After they passed a sign that read MIDDLE WOGGLEHOLE—5 MILES, they went over a bridge supported by four huge pillars, towering above a river that flowed through a deep wooded ravine. Perched on a hill in the distance were the ruins of a castle, with a single short tower and crumbling stone walls. Suddenly, the sky was obscured by thick trees that arched over the road; it was like travelling through a dark tunnel.

When they reemerged into the sunlight, they passed a second sign, which read MIDDLE WOGGLEHOLE—FOUNDED 1014 AD.

They sped past a church with a tall square tower. Just beyond it was a wide circle of grass and flower beds, at the centre of which stood a stone column covered with intricate carvings and topped with a Celtic cross.

All the houses in Middle Wogglehole were virtually identical, with stone walls and grey slate roofs. Some had been converted into shops. On the corner was a small post office with a red letterbox outside. Septimus tooted the motorcycle's horn and waved at some women chatting on the narrow sidewalk. They waved back. At the other end of the street was the Dog and Duck pub, a whitewashed building with a colourful sign hanging over its entrance, and across the street was a car repair shop, with two old-fashioned gas pumps in front of its double doors. A bald man in blue coveralls leaned under the open hood of a small red car.

Just beyond the pub, Septimus turned the motorcycle up a narrow lane, bounded by over-grown hedges. The motorcycle came to a halt at a gate with peeling white paint. A dilapidated sign reading Ivy Cottage hung precariously from a rusty nail on the gatepost. The white plaster walls and chimney were covered in ivy. The front of the cottage had two windows with pointed arches at the top and royal-blue wooden shutters at their sides. The front door was also painted royal blue and had a small circular window at eye level. Two large clay pots overflowing with flowers stood on either side of the front doorstep.

Septimus stepped off the motorcycle and removed his helmet and goggles. Toby leapt from the sidecar, slipped through the bars of the gate and raced to the cottage door.

"Marigold," Septimus muttered as he smoothed down his thick greying hair.

"Pardon?" said Eric as he took off his helmet and laid it on the seat.

"Marigold," Septimus repeated. "I mean, Mrs. Pierce. She runs the post office and village shop. Her late husband was a major in the army, you know. She tends the garden for me. I'm always so busy. She shouldn't have closed the gate. I left it open so we could drive straight in."

With a sigh, Septimus heaved the gate to one side. Eric climbed out of the sidecar and grabbed his bag.

"Come along. Let's get you settled in. I'll put the motorbike away later."

As they walked along the path to the cottage, Eric saw a streak of light shoot across the sky.

A comet? In the middle of the day?

CHAPTER TWO

IVY COTTAGE

SEPTIMUS opened the cottage door and they stepped inside. A battered old hat and a torn jacket were hanging on a hook on the wall. The low ceiling of the living room was painted white and criss-crossed by dark wooden beams. Rickety-looking stairs led to an upper storey. Something resembling a long-handled metal detector leaned against the stairs. Eric put his bag down next to it.

"Looks like there's a package in the green-house," Septimus said, peering out the kitchen window. "I'll go get it."

Eric waited by the back door while Septimus collected a small parcel from a wooden shelf just inside the greenhouse. The rear garden of the cottage had a lawn, a few flower beds and an overgrown hedge. Next to the greenhouse was a whitewashed stone building, with double doors on the front and a smaller door on the side. A narrow path of stone slabs led up to it from the cottage.

"The postman always leaves packages in the greenhouse," Septimus explained, walking back. "They're too big to fit through the letter slot on the front door."

"Is that another house?" Eric asked, pointing to the whitewashed building.

"Oh no, that's my workshop. I like to tinker with things, machinery and whatnot, you know. Nothing too complicated. It's a bit of a mess in there. There's dangerous equipment around. I don't want you getting hurt, so don't go in there, please. Your mother will be very upset with me if anything happens to you."

"Sure," said Eric with a shrug.

"Tell you what, why don't I show you up to your room? Follow me."

Eric followed his father through the kitchen and up the narrow staircase, picking his bag up on the way. At the top of the stairs, Septimus stepped through a low doorway. "This is your room."

It was tiny and sparsely furnished. Apart from the bed, there was a dresser, a bedside table with a small green lamp and a mirror in a wooden frame.

"Well, I'll leave you to it," said Septimus, pulling the drapes open. "It's a little chilly, don't you think? Why don't I go down and light a nice fire? Sort out your things, then come downstairs." Septimus backed out of the room, bumping his head on the door frame as he left.

Eric unzipped his bag and unpacked. The room was strangely cold for July, so he slipped on a sweatshirt and walked over to the window. The room overlooked the rear garden. Ivy Cottage was built on a hill, and in the distance Eric could see the bridge where they'd crossed the river that snaked through the ravine. The workshop clung precariously to the edge of a rocky cliff that dropped away sharply. Septimus was pushing his old motorcycle into the workshop.

Eric scarcely knew his father. His parents had

separated when he was very young, and Eric lived in London with his mother.

Eric shivered again and decided to go downstairs. In the sitting room, a fire was already crackling. He stood close to it to warm up. A grandfather clock stood ticking by the room's only window. Eric looked around the room. There was a very full bookcase and a worn armchair on the opposite side of the fireplace. A wicker rack filled with newspapers and magazines stood at the edge of the hearth. Eric didn't see a computer, TV or even a radio anywhere.

A strange-looking object lay on top of a glass cabinet. It looked like an egg whisk, but attached to one end was a small black plastic box with a dial. Wires of all colours protruded from it. An empty pocket-watch case sat beside it, its parts strewn around haphazardly. Eric picked up a crumpled piece of paper, but he couldn't make out what the handwritten notes, symbols and numbers meant.

On the mantle were lots of photographs in silver frames of landscapes or coastal scenes.

One photograph depicted a younger Septimus and Eric's mother at a seaside resort.

"I hope you're settling in," said Septimus. He was carrying a small tray. "I brought you a cheese sandwich and a glass of warm milk."

Septimus set the tray down on the copper-topped coffee table in front of the couch.

"Thanks," said Eric, sitting down.

"Oh my!" Septimus exclaimed, glancing over at the top of the nearby cabinet. "I didn't realize I'd left that stuff lying around." He quickly scooped up the pieces of the pocket watch, grabbed the odd-looking whisk and shoved everything into his blazer pockets.

"Just a little something I've been working on. Yes, that's it. Well, I suppose I should leave you in peace. I do have a few things to do in the workshop. Help yourself to anything in the fridge."

Septimus shuffled out of the room, muttering to himself.

The sandwich didn't look very appetizing, but tasted better than Eric had expected. After he drank the warm milk, he curled up on the couch.

Flames danced in the fireplace.

Half-asleep, Eric thought he saw a face appear in the fire. Then a blue-green flame jumped out and turned into a tiny human shape. Its solid black eyes scanned the room, its head tilting to one side as it looked at Eric.

I must be dreaming.

The figure then leapt onto the arm of the couch, reached out and touched Eric's wrist.

Eric stirred, opening his eyes wide, and the figure disappeared back into the fire.

CHAPTER THREE

MIDDLE WOGGLEHOLE

ERIC awoke on the couch the next morning with a blanket over him. Sunlight poured into the room. He winced in pain and noticed a burn mark on his right wrist.

Eric followed the smell of bacon wafting in from the kitchen. Septimus stood in front of the stove, whistling. He was wearing a gaudy red, green and yellow plaid apron.

"Oh!" he exclaimed. "I didn't see you there, Eric. Good morning. I trust you slept well? I didn't have the heart to wake you last night. You must be exhausted from your journey. A long train ride like that would wear anyone out." Septimus pointed at Eric's wrist. "Looks like you got a cinder burn from the fireplace. I've had those before."

"Yeah, can I have some ice?"

"Oh, of course," Septimus said, taking the ice tray from the freezer. He cracked the tray on the edge of the counter and handed a cube to Eric.

"Thanks. That bacon smells good. I'm hungry."

"It's almost noon," Septimus said, scooping up the bacon and sliding it onto a plate. "I've scrambled some eggs, and there's a veritable mountain of toast."

At that moment, two slices of bread popped out of the toaster beside the kettle. Septimus caught them in mid-air and began to wave them back and forth, as if conducting an orchestra.

"Fastest way to cool them down," he said with a smile.

Eric sat down at the table and buttered some toast.

"By the way, your mother called. She wanted to make sure you'd arrived safely."

Septimus took off the apron and hung it up. Just then, a shrill voice called out from the back garden. "Anyone home?"

"Marigold," said Septimus under his breath, rolling his eyes.

The door opened and a woman stepped into the kitchen. She was wearing a colourful flower-print dress and a floppy wide-brimmed hat.

"Good morning!" she cried. "You must be Eric."

She extended her hand to him. Mrs. Pierce was wearing very strong perfume.

"Beautiful day, isn't it? I'm Marigold Pierce. I'm so pleased to meet you."

"Nice to meet you too," replied Eric, shaking her hand.

"I see he's looking after you," said Mrs. Pierce. "I can't remember the last time he had guests."

"Yes, yes," Septimus sputtered. "Very good, very good. Thank you, Mrs. Pierce."

Mrs. Pierce gave him a broad smile.

"I'll go and see to the flowers then," she said. "Nice to meet you, Eric."

She picked up a small watering can from beside the sink and went out into the garden.

"Is she your girlfriend?" Eric asked between bites of bacon and eggs.

Septimus blushed. "Oh, er, she's, well . . . hmnn . . ."

Eric chuckled. "I think I'll go and explore the village a little," he said, wiping his face with a napkin.

"Good idea," said Septimus, nodding his head. "Fresh air and all that, eh? I'm afraid there aren't any children around. This place is mostly just for retired people now, living a quiet life."

"When should I be back?"

"No need to be back until dinnertime."

ERIC walked down the lane into the village. The pub was opening for lunch. A man placed a sandwich board in the middle of the sidewalk, advertising the pub's lunch menu. The post office and village shop were closed. A couple of cars passed each other on the main street, but otherwise Middle Wogglehole was virtually deserted.

Eric walked by the car repair shop and noticed a bright-red vintage English sports car with its hood up. A radio was playing, but the workshop appeared empty.

"Hello?" Eric called, looking at the car. "Anyone here?"

"Hello there," someone said.

A young girl came out from the back, wiping her hands on a rag. "Can I help you?" she asked. She was wearing thick-framed glasses and her hair was tied back in a short ponytail. There were oil and grease stains on both sides of her face and her blue coveralls were filthy.

"This is a really nice car," Eric said.

The girl stood next to Eric and hung the rag on the hood.

"Yes it is," she said. "It's a 1959 Austin-Healey Mark I. You're the boy from London, aren't you?"

"Yeah," said Eric. "How did you know?"

"The accent, mostly," she said with a grin. "You're staying with Mr. Trinket, aren't you?"

"Yeah, he's my dad. I'm Eric." He extended his hand.

"Oh, I didn't know Mr. Trinket had a son," she said, shaking it. "I'm Jessica. Are you here all summer?"

She took off her glasses. She had beautiful brown eyes, and for a moment Eric just stared.

"Safety glasses," said Jessica. "I only wear

them when I'm working on the cars."

"Oh, yeah, right," said Eric.

"So you're here all summer?" Jessica asked him again.

"Yeah," Eric replied. "Is there anything to do around here?"

"Not really. Middle Wogglehole is pretty boring."

"So what do you do all summer in a place like this?"

"Oh, I don't live here," explained Jessica. "I'm just really interested in cars. Mick—that's the owner—he's an old friend of my dad's. Mick lets me help out in the summer. I'm here three or four days a week during school holidays. Wait here a minute. I have to go and get cleaned up. I'll be right back."

She disappeared through a door behind the counter. Eric sat down on a chair and examined the faded posters of vintage cars on the walls.

A bald man came up beside him. "Hello there," he said. It was the same man Eric had seen on his way through the village the day before.

"Hi," said Eric.

"Hello, Mick," said Jessica as she came back through the door.

She'd washed the grime off her face and changed into a plain white T-shirt and blue jeans. Her short brown hair hung over her shoulders.

"This is Eric," she told Mick. "He's staying with Mr. Trinket for the summer."

"Ah, the inventor," said Mick, nodding his head. "I wonder how he keeps up that old motorbike. It's never been in here for a tune-up or anything. He tinkers with all kinds of things in that workshop of his."

"I thought I'd take a break and show Eric around."

"No problem. Actually, it's pretty quiet around here. You might as well take the afternoon off. See you tomorrow."

"We'll go to the Sentinel," Jessica said, turning to Eric.

"The what?"

"The Sentinel. It's what they call the big stone pillar on the village green."

CHAPTER FOUR

THE MYSTIC TRIANGLE

ERIC and Jessica strolled down the main street of the village. Middle Wogglehole was very quiet. There were only a couple of cars parked on the street. The sidewalks were empty except for an old man putting a bunch of envelopes in the mailbox.

"This is the village green," Jessica said when they got to the Sentinel.

The Sentinel was an eight-foot-tall stone column, featuring Christian symbols and Latin inscriptions. At the edges there was a series of short twisting lines, dashes and dots.

Eric ran his fingers over the odd markings, which were smooth from centuries of weathering. *This must be some kind of writing.* Suddenly he remembered the figure of blue-and-green flames, and pulled his hand away in alarm. He stepped back from the column, stumbling into a flower bed.

"Are you all right?" Jessica asked, extending a hand.

"Yeah. I'm just a bit dizzy, no problem."

They sat down on a bench next to the monument.

"So why is this thing called the Sentinel?"

"It guards against evil spirits. A long, long time ago, this stone was sacred to the Celts. They were pagans. After Christianity came to Britain, the Church carved Latin stuff over all the pagan monuments. They also filled in the healing spring."

"Healing spring? You mean, like magic? You've got to be kidding."

"They built the church right over it." Jessica gestured toward the houses around them. "This village has been here for a long time."

"It says a thousand years on the sign."

"People have been living here a lot longer than that. Before the castle was built, there was a Roman fort, and before that, a pagan temple. Even now, the locals still tell all sorts of old legends. Like the one about the Mystic Triangle."

"What's that?" Eric asked.

"If you connect the castle, the healing spring and the Sentinel, it makes a triangle with fantastic power."

"Do you really believe all that stuff?"

"Well, yeah," said Jessica. "Everyone in Middle Wogglehole does. This is one of the most mysterious places in England. It's in all the travel books."

"Maybe they're just trying to attract tourists."

"If they are," said Jessica, "it's not working very well, is it?"

They both laughed.

"Come on," Jessica said, "I'll show you some other places."

They walked past the Dog and Duck pub.

"This was a favourite of eighteenth-century highwaymen like Dick Turpin."

"What about Robin Hood, did he ever come here?"

"Maybe, but lots of the small towns in the north of England claim him."

They turned down School Lane.

"That was the school," said Jessica, pointing to a stone building with large windows and the same grey slate roof as most of the village houses. "It closed down about twenty years ago. They use it as a community centre now."

As they approached the end of the street, another comet streaked across the sky.

"Did you see that?" Eric said, pointing up.

Just then a small white car blared its horn and screeched to a halt in front of them. Jessica abruptly pulled Eric onto the sidewalk.

"Careful!" she exclaimed. "This might be a pretty dull place, but you still need to watch out for cars."

At the end of School Lane, they stopped in front of the church.

"St. Thomas' was built in the 1350s," Jessica said, easing open the weathered wooden gate and stepping into the churchyard. "But there were at least two churches on the site of the spring before this one, maybe more."

There were plenty of very old headstones in the churchyard. Some dated back to the 1600s.

The church itself was a tall imposing building of dark stone. The front door creaked as Jessica pushed it open. Inside the church were rows of dark wooden benches, flanked by a number of thick stone columns. High arches supported the roof. Stained-glass windows with colourful biblical scenes glowed in the sunlight.

"That's the minister," Jessica whispered, pointing to a man in a black cassock. He was sorting through some prayer books on a shelf at the base of the ornately carved wooden pulpit.

They walked over to a slab of stone just inside the doorway. Carved into the top was an effigy of a knight in armour, with a sword at his side. Eric gazed at the carved stone face in the half-light, and for a fleeting second he thought it came to life—a man with white hair, a thick beard and blue-green wrinkled skin. Eric stepped back, startled, and tipped over a bench. The crash echoed through the empty church.

"Are you all right?" asked Jessica.

"Yeah, I'm fine."

"Are you sure? You look like you've seen a ghost."

"Yeah. Yeah, I'm sure," Eric replied, although he wasn't entirely convinced. He glanced at the knight, but the face had turned back to stone.

The church bell struck four times as they walked out into the sun.

"Wow," said Jessica, "four o'clock already. I'd better be getting back. My dad's picking me up soon. We could meet up tomorrow and walk up to the castle, if you like. You get an amazing view for miles around."

"Sounds great."

"Shall we meet around ten o'clock, at the repair shop?" suggested Jessica.

"Sure, that'll be fun. See you tomorrow."

Eric began to think that Middle Wogglehole might not be such a dull place to spend the summer after all.

CHAPTER FIVE

DREAMING IN DUPLICATE

"UTTER nonsense," Septimus scoffed, scooping some more mashed potatoes onto Eric's plate.

"I dunno," said Eric, "she was pretty convinced."

"Well, there are a lot of legends here. But all this talk about magic, superstitious claptrap, that's what it is." He tossed a scrap of meat to Toby, who gobbled it up.

"We're going up to the castle tomorrow," said Eric, yawning.

"Still tired, eh?" said Septimus.

"I didn't sleep well last night. I had a weird dream."

"Weird dream?"

Toby perked up his ears and whined.

"There was a kind of a fire person . . . it came

out of the fireplace and touched my wrist. Right here," he added, pointing to his burn.

Toby snorted and began pacing back and forth.

"Sit down and eat your scraps, Toby. You're making me nervous."

Toby crawled under the table and covered his eyes with a paw.

"Don't worry, Eric," said Septimus. "Dreams don't usually mean anything. Just get some sleep. I have to go out early in the morning. I'll leave you a key on the table." He looked under the table at Toby, considering something. "Why don't you take Toby with you when you go to the castle? He likes to get out."

"Sure."

"His leash is just over by the back door. You'll only need it when you're near the road. You can let him run free otherwise."

"Okay," said Eric, finishing his potatoes. "And thanks for dinner."

"You're most welcome," Septimus replied with a brief bow. "Get some rest and I'll see you when you get back from your walk tomorrow."

ERIC woke up thirsty in the middle of the night. He went downstairs to get a drink of water and noticed a fluctuating light coming from behind the kitchen door.

Septimus' voice came through the door. "I think I have it this time."

A different voice replied, "You said that before."

"I know what I'm doing," Septimus said. "It doesn't like you very much, you know that. Now, let me concentrate."

The door was slightly ajar, and Eric pushed it open just enough to peek into the kitchen. Septimus was seated at the kitchen table with Toby at his feet. A blue crystal sphere, small enough to fit in the palm of Eric's hand, rested on the table. It pulsated with a faint blue-green light. Next to it was a large ceramic bowl and jug.

Septimus stood up from the table, lifted the jug and poured water into the bowl, filling it to the brim. He picked up the glowing sphere and held it above the water. Then he let it go, but the sphere didn't fall. It hung suspended in the air.

Then the light faded. The kitchen was shrouded

in darkness. Glittering stars appeared inside the sphere. Then images of people, buildings and strange creatures, the likes of which Eric had never seen before, rose from the water and drifted around the room. Septimus stroked his beard. Suddenly there was a blinding flash and everything went black.

DID I dream that? Eric thought when he woke up the next morning. *It was so real.* Eric got dressed and went downstairs. Toby was curled up on the couch and there was no sign of Septimus. Eric made himself a couple of slices of toast and wolfed them down. Toby came into the kitchen and stood beside the leash. Eric picked it up, attached it to Toby's collar, then took the key from the kitchen table and headed out.

Jessica was waiting for him beside the gas pumps.

"Hi," Eric called as he approached.

"Morning. Is this your dad's dog?"

"Yeah," said Eric, "I promised I'd bring him along. I hope you don't mind."

"No, that's fine." Jessica reached down to stroke Toby's head, but he growled and she pulled her hand back.

"Sorry. I don't think he's very friendly."

"Never mind. Come on, there's a path not far from the church that leads up to the castle."

Eric let Toby off the leash once they were safely on the path. Along the way, Jessica talked about the history of the castle.

"Here we are," she announced when they reached the top of the path.

It hadn't taken them long to reach the ruins. The view from the top of the hill was indeed spectacular. Eric could make out parts of the winding road that led to the village, as well as the bridge spanning the gorge. He could see the village's main street, the church and the Sentinel. He could also see Ivy Cottage, perched on a craggy hill, looking very isolated from the rest of the village.

Most of the castle's main tower had broken down, and its crumbling stone walls had been overgrown with grass and weeds. Toby started sniffing around and disappeared behind the rubble.

"Careful," said Jessica when Eric jumped between two rocks. "Watch out for the ring."

"What ring?"

"You're standing right over the entrance to a fairy ring. It's best to avoid it."

"Okay, okay," Eric muttered, stepping to one side. "Fairy rings, fire creatures, this place is crazy."

"What did you say?"

"Oh, nothing." Eric sat down under a tree. "I had a weird dream last night. There was this glowing sphere or something, and it floated. And the night before that, I had a dream about a creature that came out of the fire and burned my wrist."

Jessica sat down beside him. "You're not the only one. I've heard people talking at the pumps. Everyone in Middle Wogglehole seems to be having strange dreams."

"Really?" Eric felt very uneasy.

"Maybe it has something to do with the Mystic Triangle."

"My dad said all that stuff is superstitious rubbish."

"Did he now?" Jessica said with a grin. "Well I know he spends a lot of time up here at the castle. I've seen him over at the church and the Sentinel too. He's always measuring things. And of course, there are all those odd stories about that cottage of his."

"That's weird. Hey—where's Toby?"

"There he is!"

Toby raced away from the castle down a different path.

"Quick! After him!"

CHAPTER SIX

THE WORKSHOP

ERIC and Jessica chased Toby down the path until they ended up on the lane to Ivy Cottage. But there was no sign of him.

"Where'd he go?" Eric asked, panting. "He was just here."

They hurried around the side of the cottage and into the garden, but there was still no sign of Toby.

"Hey, look," said Jessica, pointing at the workshop. "The side door's open. Maybe he went in there? We should check."

"My dad told me not to go in his workshop," Eric said. "He said it's dangerous."

"We'll just take a quick look. We won't touch anything."

They peered through the open door into the workshop. "Toby? Are you in there?" called Eric.

"Come on," said Jessica, "let's look inside."

She pushed past Eric and flicked on the lights. Pieces of machinery cluttered up every corner. The shelves along the walls were filled with plastic bottles of motor oil, toolboxes, rusty cans and glass jars.

At the back were two wide wooden tables. One of them was littered with crystals of all sizes and jars of coloured liquid, metal coins, antique jewellery and small weapons. The other overflowed with books, magazines and newspaper clippings.

Jessica picked up a clipping. "'Two New Fairy Rings Discovered in Derbyshire,'" she read aloud.

Eric opened a magazine. "'Middle Wogglehole: Most Magical Place in England.'"

A large leather-bound volume lay open on the table. Eric flipped through page after page of pictures of monuments and ancient artifacts. "Look, the writing here is just like the carvings on the Sentinel."

"It's Celtic script," said Jessica. "I studied that stuff for a school project."

"What does it say?"

"How should I know? I wonder what he has all this for?"

"Yeah. He told me all those legends and things are nonsense."

Eric picked up a small dagger from the other table and studied the unusual script on the handle. It was just like the writing in the old book. "This stuff looks like it belongs in a museum."

"Look at this," Jessica said. "I think it's the Mystic Triangle." She handed Eric a diagram covered in scribbled notes and equations.

"Wow, you're right," said Eric. Then he picked up a small blue crystal sphere. "What's this?"

Suddenly there was an ear-splitting clap of thunder. Eric followed Jessica outside. A whirlpool of black clouds swirled high in the sky above the castle. Lightning flashed back and forth at the whirlpool's centre.

"What the heck is that?" cried Jessica, mesmerized.

The crystal sphere in Eric's palm pulsated with light. "It's glowing," he said.

The sphere shone brighter and brighter. Then the air rippled and opened up, revealing a city skyline of towers, pyramids and spires. Strange winged creatures flew above the city. A bolt of lightning struck the slate roof of the workshop, and Eric turned around.

"Eric!" Jessica screamed.

By the time he turned back, the strange city was gone. So was Jessica.

"Jessica! Where are you?"

There was no answer. Eric searched frantically over the cliff edge, but there was no sign of her, only the roar of an engine. The sphere was no longer glowing.

Septimus' motorcycle screeched to a halt beside Eric. Toby was sitting calmly in the sidecar.

"Jessica . . ." Eric gasped, barely able to speak. "She—she disappeared."

Toby turned to Septimus and said, "You had better tell him everything."

CHAPTER SEVEN

SEPTIMUS' SECRET

"COME inside," said Septimus as he stepped off the motorcycle and headed for the cottage door. Toby trailed behind.

Eric followed him into the kitchen. He was still clutching the sphere.

"Try to remain calm," Septimus said. He nodded to Toby.

Toby stood up on his hind legs and began to grow taller. His front and rear paws morphed into clawed and hairy hands and feet. His thick fur turned into an armoured breastplate and a long chain-mail shirt that hung down to his knees. The leather collar around his neck became a decorative band, bedecked with jewels, and thick silver bracelets covered both his wrists.

He stood six feet tall, towering over Eric—a

dog's head on a humanoid body, all covered with black hair. "Greetings, young man. My name is Tobias."

Eric stared at him open-mouthed.

"Don't be afraid," said Septimus. "He won't bite."

Tobias shot Septimus a frosty look. He extended his clawed hand, and Eric shook it gingerly.

It was a while before Eric could say anything. "Where's Jessica?" he finally demanded.

"She is in our world now," Septimus replied gravely.

"What do you mean, 'our world'?"

Septimus and Tobias looked at each other.

"Septimus and I are from Koronada," said Tobias. "Koronada is in another universe."

"Would you like a glass of water, Eric?" Septimus asked.

Eric nodded slowly as he placed the sphere on the table. Septimus filled a glass with water and handed it to Eric, who drained it in three gulps.

Tobias pointed to the symbol on his breastplate. "This is the emblem of the province of Tekara. Your father and I were once proud to serve Galderon, the guardian of our province. I was Lord Protector."

"And I was Tekara's Grand Magus," said Septimus, "a kind of chief magician and inventor."

"This is all very confusing."

"On occasion throughout history, unstable portals have appeared, creating fleeting, temporary doorways between the universes."

"What do you mean?"

"Sometimes Earth creatures slip into our world through one of the unstable portals," Tobias replied, "like Jessica did. It happens the other way around, too; hence the legends of strange creatures on Earth. One of my ancestors slipped through a portal into ancient Egypt before the time of the pharaohs, and he was welcomed as a god. They called him Anubis."

"That's crazy. How did you get to Earth? What happened?"

"Galderon was once a good leader," said Septimus. "But he became power hungry after I created a sphere that allowed him to open doorways to other worlds. He declared a war on the other provinces, and appointed himself Emperor of Koronada."

"Septimus and I joined the Brotherhood of the Fallen in the war against Galderon, so he cast us through a portal," said Tobias. "We ended up here."

"And Jessica is there, in that terrible place?"

"I'm afraid so, Eric," Septimus said. "But we can go back there and help her."

"How?"

Septimus pointed at the sphere on the table. "With that. Tobias and I couldn't get it to work for us, but it opened a portal for you. Maybe you'll be able to do it."

"What did you do to get the sphere to work?" Tobias said.

"I didn't do anything," Eric replied. "It just kind of happened, then she was gone."

"You must remember," said Tobias. "We may already be too late."

"What do you mean?" Eric asked.

"The dream you had, with the fire creature. It was a projection of Galderon himself," Septimus explained. "Like the energy flashes above the castle. Galderon is learning how to manipulate the sphere I made for him. That was my mistake. The power of the sphere turned him into a monster."

"And he's trying to invade Earth?"

"He wants to take over everything, every universe," said Tobias. "So far he has not succeeded."

"We need to move quickly," Septimus said as he picked up the sphere from the table. "Jessica is in danger in Koronada. We have to act fast. I know what to do."

Tobias turned back into Toby the dog and ran outside to the motorcycle. Eric clambered into the sidecar behind Toby. Septimus drove the motorcycle across the back lawn and stopped beside the greenhouse.

"What are you doing?" said Eric.

"You'll see," said Septimus.

He turned off the engine and pulled a crumpled piece of paper from his pocket.

"Wait here," he said to Eric and Toby.

He climbed off the motorcycle and walked across to the edge of the cliff. In the sky, bolts of lightning flashed in a black whirlpool of clouds.

Septimus held the sheet of paper out and studied it closely.

"Just doing a final check," he said, walking back. "Tobias and I first arrived here at Ivy Cottage years ago. The place had been empty for a long time. Ivy Cottage is at the centre of the Mystic Triangle. So we knew the portal would be right here.

"We could see through this portal into Koronada, but neither Tobias nor I have been able to pass through it until now." Septimus nodded at Eric. "But that's about to change."

The storm was growing worse. In a field at the edge of the village, a bolt of lightning hit a tree, setting it alight.

Septimus handed Eric the sphere.

"What do I do?"

"Just hold tight. The sphere should do the rest."

The sphere began to glow brightly and pulsate in Eric's hand. Directly in front of him, the air began to shimmer.

"There it is!" said Toby. "We must hurry."

"Hold on tight," Septimus said. He started

the motorcycle and twisted the throttle as far as it would go. The motorcycle and sidecar roared across the lawn toward the cliff, and flew into the air. Eric screamed as they dropped into the ravine like a stone. Then suddenly the portal opened and the ravine vanished before their eyes.

CHAPTER EIGHT

THE MALKONOR STRIKES

ERIC was still screaming when the motorcycle hit the ground with a thud. They were in the middle of a thick forest. Eric pulled off his helmet and tossed it to the ground, then scrambled out of the sidecar. Toby transformed back into Tobias.

"Is anyone hurt?" Tobias asked.

"No, I don't think so," replied Septimus, rubbing his head. "Just a little sore."

"We are home," Tobias said with a smile. "Welcome to Koronada."

"We need to get away from here," said Septimus, "in case our arrival has been noticed. Galderon's agents are everywhere."

"Garoda is not too far from here," said Tobias. "We should head there to find out if anyone has seen Jessica."

"Let's hide the motorcycle first," Septimus said.

They pushed the motorcycle into a thicket and covered everything with branches.

"Put the sphere in your pocket, Eric," said Septimus, "and don't show it to anyone."

SPREAD along a coastline, beside a shimmering blue sea, was the city Eric had glimpsed in the portal back on Earth, right before Jessica disappeared. Stepped pyramids and spires dominated the skyline. Many of the buildings were severely damaged and others were little more than ruins.

Suddenly there was a loud screech and Eric looked up. Large, dark-grey creatures with bat-like wings soared in the sky above.

"Scarans," Tobias muttered.

"What?" said Eric.

"Scarans," Tobias repeated. "One of the many creatures that now serve Galderon. Come, we need to reach the city as quickly as we can."

The three travellers followed a deserted road that led to the open gates of Garoda. It looked like a medieval city, with crowds milling about. Some of the creatures resembled humans, but on closer inspection Eric saw that they were very different. Some had oddly shaped ears; others had strange skulls; many had small antennae, short horns or blue, green or purple skin. There were other beings, half-human, half-beast like Tobias—reptiles, lions, tigers, bears, rhinos. Some were old and some were young. Some wore armoured breastplates emblazoned with a variety of crests, and carried swords. Others wore thigh-length tunics, narrow leggings and lightweight leather boots. Pouches hung from belts around their waists. The children wore sandals, and the females' dresses hung down to their ankles. Some had veils or other head coverings, while others wore their hair loose or tightly braided. A handful were dressed in bright colours.

There were many animals too. They were a little like horses, or cows, or sheep or goats, but not quite. They drank from the river near an enormous waterwheel.

The streets were paved with large stone slabs, and the buildings that were still intact had white plastered walls. The writing on the shop signs was just like the inscriptions Eric had seen in Septimus' workshop.

"Is that Celtic writing?" Eric asked.

"It certainly is," said Septimus with a smile.

They walked along the riverbank until they reached the harbour. The remains of huge monuments barely jutted above the surface of the water, like bizarrely shaped islands. A handful of small boats drifted between them. Rubble from half-crumbled buildings littered the edge of the harbour.

"What happened here?" Eric asked.

"Galderon's revenge," replied Tobias. "The siege of Garoda lasted for many months. Septimus and I were able to watch some of the events from Earth, using the sphere. The harbour was the pride of the city, surrounded by beautiful buildings, historic palaces and the tombs and mausoleums of the guardians. Now all that is gone. My wife and children were caught up in the fighting. I still do not know if they survived."

"I hope they did," Eric said.

"You two carry on," said Tobias. "I need to find the Brotherhood. They will have news of the war."

"And Jessica," Septimus added.

"Take this," said Tobias, handing Septimus a small leather purse. "The two of you need to change into Garodan clothes. There should be enough coins in here to buy some clothing and a meal. Meet me at the marketplace at sundown."

Tobias disappeared into the crowd.

Septimus led Eric to a small shop in a narrow alley. They bought some clothes, changed, and decided to look for an inn where they could have something to eat. They'd only taken a few steps out of the alley when Eric nearly bumped into a watch with bright-red skin.

"A malkonor," said Septimus, pulling Eric away. "I was hoping word of our arrival wouldn't have spread so quickly."

"You must come with me—and the boy, too,"

said the red-skinned creature, holding up his hand. His eyes were yellow, with thin black pupils. "Galderon has summoned you."

The creature grew, his flesh turning reptilian, with shiny red scales. At the same time, his face stretched into a crocodile snout, dripping with green saliva. His long forked tongue flickered between his teeth. His fingers and toes grew long claws, and two short horns appeared on his head. The malkonor grew ten feet tall, a ridge of spikes rose along his spine and he sprouted a tail with a bony club at its end. He raised his tail and brought the club crashing to the ground.

"You can come with me willingly . . . or not," snarled the malkonor, narrowing his eyes. He took a step forward, and wisps of grey smoke seeped out from his nostrils.

"Get behind me," said Septimus.

"What?" Eric stammered, scarcely able to take his eyes off the malkonor. His pulse raced.

"Quick!" Septimus snapped.

Eric jumped behind him. Before Septimus could do anything, the malkonor opened his jaws.

With a thunderous roar he shot a blast of fire, and Septimus disappeared in a ball of flame.

"Stay exactly where you are, boy," the malkonor ordered, licking his lips.

Eric turned and ran. He raced back down the alley, through a busy street and into another alley. But two men, one with long dark hair and a beard, the other one bald, blocked his exit.

"Don't worry," said the bearded man, edging closer, "we're not going to hurt you."

"We're going to help you," the bald man added, taking a step forward. "Come with us."

Eric panicked. He turned and ran back down the alley, into a courtyard, and right into a stack of wooden crates. The men were right behind him.

"Quiet!" hissed the bearded man, placing his hand over Eric's mouth and pinning his arm to a wall. "They'll hear you."

The bald man grabbed Eric's other arm. Eric could hardly breathe, his eyes wide with fear. A stunning woman with pure white hair that hung down to her waist came out of a doorway. She wore a purple robe with a golden sash.

"Leave him to me," she said, reaching out to Eric and touching his forehead. Eric was mesmerized by her purple eyes.

The woman gently passed her hand down Eric's face.

"Sleep," she said softly. "Sleep."

The last thing Eric saw was her beautiful face. Then everything went dark.

CHAPTER NINE

REUNION

"ERIC, are you okay?"

"Jessica?" said Eric, slowly opening his eyes.

They were on the coast, at the edge of a forest. The waves were lapping up against the sandy driftwood-strewn beach. It was still light but darkness was falling. There were two full moons in the sky just above the horizon, one slightly larger than the other.

"There was a ball of flame . . ."

"It's okay, Eric. Kilaya's told me everything."

The woman with the purple eyes came up to him.

"Eric, this is Kilaya," said Jessica.

"Where are we?" asked Eric. "What did you do to me?"

"We're your friends, Eric. We're here to help

you. I'm sorry I had to put you to sleep back there in the alley."

"My dad . . . Septimus, is he . . . dead?"

"We think so," said Kilaya. "Malkonors have no pity. There's nothing you could have done to help him."

Eric sighed. *I wish I'd known him better.*

"I'm so sorry, Eric," said Kilaya, placing a reassuring hand on his forearm.

Jessica gave him a hug. "He was a good man. Everyone in the village liked him, even if they thought he was a little crazy."

"Does Tobias know? He was going to meet me and Septimus at the marketplace."

"He's coming here tomorrow," Kilaya said. "We'll tell him then."

"My mom will want to know about it too." Then Eric remembered the sphere, and patted his pocket. *It's gone!* Without it he couldn't get back to Earth.

"It's all right, Eric," said Kilaya. "Jessica has the sphere."

How did she know what I was thinking?

"Why don't the two of you go over to the fire? It's getting a little cool. I'll bring you dinner."

The camp was in a small clearing in the middle of a thick grove of trees. Several campfires were lit, and Eric recognized many of the different races he'd seen in Garoda. There were dozens of canopies supported by poles and broken branches, and small tents were scattered about the clearing. One large dark-green tent stood at a far edge.

Eric and Jessica sat down by one of the fires. Kilaya handed each of them some bread and a bowl of hot soup with chunks of meat.

"What's in this?" Eric asked.

"Don't worry," said Jessica, "it tastes just like chicken."

The two men who had captured Eric approached the campfire.

"Eric," said Kilaya, "this is Alcamarus, and his brother, Soldor."

They had swords and long-bladed knives sheathed at their belts. Their armoured breast-plates were similar to Tobias', but displayed a different symbol.

"Alcamarus is one of our leaders," Kilaya said. "He and Soldor command our army."

Eric stood up and shook their hands. Alcamarus had shoulder length black hair, a neatly trimmed beard and a friendly face. Soldor was completely bald and looked far more menacing. He had a deep scar running down the right side of his face and was missing part of his ear.

"I'm sorry if we scared you in the alley," said Alcamarus, smiling.

"It was necessary," Soldor added.

"We're the Brotherhood of the Fallen," said Alcamarus. "We're the only ones still resisting Galderon's rule."

"Galderon's sphere grants him great power," said Soldor. "He's taken control of the most vicious creatures of our world to help him win. There are hardly any birds left because of the scarans. And the malkonors have devastated the unicorn herds."

Alcamarus turned to Kilaya. "We need to talk."

"And Karonvar would like to see the children in the morning too," Soldor said.

Kilaya walked off with Alcamarus and Soldor to the edge of the clearing. Jessica and Eric were left alone beside the fire.

"Who's Karonvar?" asked Eric.

"The leader of the Brotherhood." Jessica took a sip of her soup.

"And what about Kilaya?"

"She's Karonvar's closest advisor. She's a telepath. By the way, I'm so sorry about Septimus," she said.

"There was no time to do anything. He probably never knew what hit him." Eric looked down and took a bite of bread, trying to drive the image from his mind. He shuddered before regaining his composure. "So . . . um . . . what happened to you when you vanished from the cottage?" He hoped Jessica couldn't see the tears in his eyes.

"Well, I appeared in the woods just outside Garoda," Jessica replied. "That's one of the portals here. I was scared, of course, not knowing what was going on. Luckily, some of the Brotherhood were patrolling that area. They found me before Galderon's monsters did and brought me to the camp. The Brotherhood gave me these clothes and helped me to settle in here. Kilaya told me that they have to move camps quite often, but this one in the Forest of Orbann is quite secure."

"Tobias told me something about the Brotherhood."

Jessica took the blue sphere out of her pocket and handed it to Eric. "Kilaya says the sphere has incredible powers, in the right hands."

"I'll take good care of it."

"Now let's get some rest," said Jessica. "The days are long here. I'll show you where we'll sleep."

As Eric was falling asleep that night, his thoughts kept returning to the horrific moment when the ball of flame consumed Septimus.

CHAPTER TEN

THE BROTHERHOOD OF THE FALLEN

ERIC awoke to brilliant sunshine the next morning after a restless night's sleep, and the events of the previous day came back to him. *Septimus . . . Dad.*

"About time you woke up," said Jessica.

The camp was a hive of activity, with far more people around than the night before. A creature with a long tail and wide, transparent dragonfly wings flew into the centre of the camp. She had pale-green skin and short black hair, and was clad in a short white robe. Alcamarus and Soldor walked up to her. The three of them crossed the camp and disappeared into a dark-green tent.

"That's Zaliya," said Jessica. "She's a friend of

Karonvar. She must have some news. But never mind that. Kilaya has breakfast ready for us, and I'm hungry."

Eric followed Jessica to a canopy strung between two stout oak trees.

"Good morning, Eric," Kilaya said. "I hope you slept well."

"Yeah . . . well, sort of." Eric sat down.

Breakfast consisted of a kind of bread and several weird types of fruit. As they ate, Eric noticed that the pendants on Kilaya's necklace had symbols like those on the armour worn by Alcamarus and Soldor.

"Eric, give me the sphere, please," Kilaya said.

Eric hesitated for a moment, then reached into his pocket and handed the sphere to Kilaya.

"This is a dangerous weapon," she said. "It can make you very powerful. That is . . . if it likes you."

"*Likes* you?" said Eric.

"The sphere has a kind of consciousness. If it likes you, it can help you do anything."

"It must like me then," said Eric, glancing at the sphere in Kilaya's hand. "But I'm not sure I like it. It's only brought me trouble."

The sphere glowed slightly, and Kilaya put it down on the grass.

"You might want to watch what you say, Eric, after what happened to Soldor."

"Yeah, it was scary," said Jessica. "Soldor wanted to use the sphere to give the warriors powers to help them in the coming battles. The sphere obviously didn't approve of that. It shot two lightning bolts at his head and only just missed."

"So if Galderon's sphere works like this one," said Eric, "his sphere must like him, right?"

"That's correct. With the help of his sphere, Galderon can do terrible things. Without it he wouldn't have been able to conquer Koronada. But we think this sphere is even more powerful— in *your* hands."

"Really?" asked Eric.

"Yes. It could be because you're from Earth." Kilaya poured water from a jug into a large wooden bowl. Then she picked up the sphere and handed it to him. "Here, Eric. See if you can make it work."

"How?" Eric asked.

"Just focus," replied Kilaya, placing the bowl of water in front of him. "Clear your mind. You too, Jessica. It might like you."

Eric held the sphere in his palm. At first nothing happened. Then suddenly he was surrounded by thick fog and mist.

"Don't be afraid, Eric. I'm here to help you."

Eric thought it was Kilaya speaking to him, but then the voice changed.

"I can be anyone you want me to be, Eric."

This time the voice reminded Eric of his mother. He knew she'd be worried about him. He never got a chance to call her like he'd promised. And now he had no idea if he'd ever get home again. Then the voice changed again.

"Or perhaps you prefer someone else?" it said in Jessica's voice.

Eric almost dropped the sphere in alarm. His heart was pounding.

"Look at the bowl, Eric. Don't be afraid."

The fog dissipated, and the sphere slowly rose out of Eric's hand and floated above the bowl.

It glowed brightly as it hovered between Eric and Jessica. In the air above the bowl, an image shimmered into view—stars swirling against a night sky. Suddenly the image changed, and a bird's head—its beak open wide—appeared, screeching. It was a tall bird with brown feathers and a huge yellow hooked beak. Instead of wings it had short arms, each tipped by a long curved claw.

"That's a terrorbird. It can't fly, but it can run very fast," said Kilaya. "It's at least ten feet tall."

The terrorbird melted away and was replaced by a large, lumbering black-haired gorilla with one eye in the middle of its forehead, and a long trunk and tusks, like an elephant. It had claws like hunting knives.

"A terexian," Kilaya said. "Its trunk can crush a grown man. They serve Galderon, just like the terrorbirds. That's enough for now."

Kilaya reached out and gently took the sphere, which immediately stopped glowing, and handed it to Eric.

Alcamarus and Zaliya came out of the green tent

and walked over to join Eric, Jessica and Kilaya.

"Eric, meet Zaliya," said Kilaya.

Zaliya's green skin had stripes, almost like a tiger's. She also had pointed ears.

"Hello, Eric," said Zaliya. The short antennae on either side of her forehead vibrated. "I'm sorry to hear about your father."

"Thanks. I'm sorry too."

Zaliya turned to Kilaya. "On my last flight I saw signs of terrorbird activity north of here."

"We've been here too long," said Alcamarus. "We have to move soon."

Zaliya turned to Eric and Jessica. "Karonvar is ready for you now."

KILAYA held open the flap of Karonvar's tent, ushered Jessica and Eric inside, then turned and left. At the far end of the tent stood Tobias. At a table next to him sat a strange creature, looking at a map. He had a goatee and jet-black hair swept back from his face. Two small horns protruded from either side of his upper forehead.

He looks like the devil!

Tobias turned to see who had come in. "Eric!" he said, hurrying over to embrace him. "I am so sorry about your father. He was a good friend."

"Yes," agreed Karonvar. "He played a big part in our early battles to regain our freedom. I was the chief advisor to Vina of Garanbal before the crisis." He pointed to the map on the table in front of him.

Eric, Jessica and Tobias sat down around the table. The map was labelled with the same Celtic symbols that Eric had seen before.

Karonvar touched each spot on the map as he spoke. "Zaliya is from Tilatt, Kilaya is from Kadosch, and Alcamarus and Soldor are from Ovolan."

"Galderon was the guardian of Tekara," said Tobias, pointing to the bottom left of the map. "Galderon defeated Kromm, then moved on to Tilatt. By the time he attacked Garanbal's territory, the other nations had formed an alliance. We are all that is left of that army."

"Look here," said Karonvar. "That's Garoda, where you all arrived through the portal. It was the last city to fall, after a long siege. Galderon killed many, and enslaved everyone who survived."

"My family was in the city during the siege," Tobias said, clearing his throat. He stood up from the table and wiped a tear from his eye. "We saw everything with Septimus' sphere. They are probably all dead—my wife, my boys, my mother, my brave father. Every one of them." He took a deep breath. "I should go now and assist Alcamarus."

Karonvar nodded and Tobias left the tent.

"Tobias misses his family," said Karonvar. "I don't know how much longer any of us in the Brotherhood will survive. We've lost so many good people."

"Like my dad," Eric said with a sigh.

Karonvar put his hand on Eric's shoulder. "Your father remained true to the cause. He was brave and selfless. But I feel we have some hope with the sphere he made. Has Kilaya told you about its abilities?"

"A little."

"Galderon will try to steal your sphere. And if

he does, he'll be able to open portals into every universe. He'll be invincible."

"Can we stop him?" Jessica said, turning to Karonvar.

"I think so. Right now we're here in Zangocia," said Karonvar, pointing at the map. "But by tomorrow we'll start moving toward the Citadel in Tekara."

Soldor rushed into tent. "Karonvar, there's a dead olokaren on the beach. It's one of the big ones."

Karonvar hurried from the tent, and Eric and Jessica followed him.

Kilaya came up to them.

"What's an olokaren?" Jessica asked.

"You need to see it for yourself," replied Kilaya.

A small crowd had gathered near the water's edge. A hideous black shape lay on the beach. It had an insect-like head, with four eyes extended on thick stalks, and multiple tentacles covered with deadly looking spikes. Its tail and flippers were similar to a whale's.

Eric took a step forward to get a better look, but Karonvar grabbed his arm.

"Don't get too close," Karonvar warned. "The shorter tentacles have mouths with razor-sharp teeth."

"But it's dead, isn't it?"

"We need to be sure." Karonvar nodded at four men armed with long spears, who took a step forward. "The olokarens attack anything that swims. They even eat each other."

Suddenly one of the olokaren's tentacles lashed out, and one of the men was bitten. He screamed in agony and collapsed, his body convulsing.

A trumpet call sounded. "The scarans!" Karonvar shouted. "Galderon has found us."

Scarans soared toward the beach, and hordes of olokarens cut through the waves. In the distance a throng of soldiers from Galderon's army were approaching from the far end of the beach.

"Kilaya, take Jessica and Eric to safety," said Karonvar. "The rest of you, come with me."

Kilaya led Eric and Jessica and a few others up the cliffs overlooking the beach. Below, the battle was raging. Galderon's troops, terexians, malkonors and terrorbirds advanced on the Brotherhood warriors. Hordes of scarans swooped down and scooped up soldiers, tossing them into the crashing waves, where the olokarens devoured them. Alcamarus and Soldor were directing their forces from the edge of the forest, but Tobias and Zaliya were nowhere in sight.

"We have to go, Eric!" said Kilaya, tugging at his arm. "We have no time to waste."

But when they turned to leave, their way was blocked by two towering terexians. One bellowed as it raised its trunk in the air, and the other glared at them with its single eye.

Suddenly there was a flash of steel as Karonvar appeared from nowhere. A single blow from his sword felled the first terexian, but the other slashed at him with its claws.

Karonvar fell but quickly scrambled to his feet. "Run!" he shouted as he struggled to protect himself with his shield. "Save yourselves!"

He dealt several blows to the terexian's trunk but that only angered the monster even more. It snatched Karonvar's shield and tossed it aside. Karonvar continued to slash at the terexian until it grabbed his sword and snapped it in two. The terexian then picked up Karonvar, crushed his ribs with its trunk and flung him over the cliff.

Jessica screamed.

"There's nothing we can do," shouted Kilaya over the terexian's roars of triumph. "We need to get out of here quickly."

CHAPTER ELEVEN

VISIONS

BY nightfall, the remnants of the Brotherhood were hidden in caves deep in the Ligordian Mountains. Zaliya and Soldor were helping some of the stragglers, but there was still no sign of Tobias.

Once everyone had gathered, Alcamarus addressed the assembled group. "I won't detain you for long. I know you're all weary from the journey. Karonvar meant so much to each of us. If it hadn't been for him, the Brotherhood wouldn't exist. He can never be replaced. We owe him everything, and I hope in my heart that I will be a worthy successor."

Everyone nodded their heads. Exhausted from the journey, they settled in for the night. Eric shared a cave with Kilaya and Jessica, and fell asleep beside a small fire.

ERIC stood in a dark circular room. At its centre was a stone archway, surrounded by stone pillars, fitted with flaming torches. The room had a ceiling but no walls, and Eric could see the night sky beyond the pillars. Septimus was chained to one of them. His face was almost drained of colour, his eyes half-closed.

As Eric approached, Septimus looked directly at him. "Eric, I'm alive," he murmured. "Help me."

Eric sat up with a start, his heart pounding. He was sweating and gasping for breath. He scrambled over to where Jessica lay on the opposite side of the fire. It was dark outside and the fire was still burning.

"Jessica," he whispered. "Wake up."

"What is it?" she asked, slowly opening her eyes. "We can't have been asleep very long."

"It's Septimus," Eric said, quietly. "He came to me in a dream."

"So?" Jessica yawned as she sat up.

"It was so vivid. He told me he's still alive."

"But didn't you say that thing shot him with a fireball?"

"I know. It's crazy."

"Your dream could have some important meaning," Kilaya interrupted.

"You're awake?"

"Of course. I rarely sleep. Where was Septimus in the dream, Eric?"

"It was dark, but there were flaming torches. There was an archway in the middle of the room."

"The Citadel," Kilaya said. "He could still be alive."

"But he can't be," insisted Eric. "I was there. I saw him burn up with my own eyes."

"Eric, it's possible that Septimus was somehow teleported to the Citadel."

Kilaya took the sphere out of her pocket and handed it to Eric. "I want you to concentrate, like you did last time. Focus on your dream, anything you can remember, no matter how insignificant it may seem. Maybe the sphere will show us what's happening."

They sat in silence. Soon the sphere pulsated gently. Eric felt completely at peace. The sphere began glowing with a pale blue-green light.

"Let go of it, Eric," Kilaya said.

"What?"

"You'll see."

Eric let it go and it slowly rose into the air, suspended above the fire. Swirling stars in a black sky filled the sphere. Soon Galderon's Citadel in Tekara appeared, steadily becoming clearer. Steep cliffs surrounded the jet-black stone fortress on all sides. It looked like it was carved right out of the cliffs. The Citadel had six tall, black pointed towers. At the top of the tallest one, a bright light was pulsating. Where the cliff face merged with its walls, there were several caves, far above the tropical forest floor. High in the sky above the Citadel, forked lightning flashed back and forth across a huge whirlpool of black clouds, just like the one back on Earth.

The image changed to a scene inside the murky walls of the Citadel. It was the same room that Eric had seen in his dream.

"Look at the archway, Eric," said Jessica. "It's another portal."

Images of herds of unicorns, soaring griffins,

and a black sky speckled with stars, planets and meteor showers flashed across the archway.

Then a figure emerged from the darkness, clad in a full suit of lightweight jet-black armour and a black cloak, fastened at the neck by an elaborate golden clasp. His hair was swept back from his blue-green face and he had a thick white beard. Eric shuddered, recalling the face he'd seen at the tomb in the church back at the village.

"Galderon," said Kilaya.

Galderon's skin was reptilian, covered in scales. His eyes were pale green with large black pupils. He had bony ridges at his eyebrows, and his ears were slightly pointed at the top and bottom. The symbol on his breastplate was the same as Tobias'.

Septimus was chained to one of the pillars. He was only semiconscious, and his face was cut and bruised.

"I warn you," Galderon snarled, carefully removing his sturdy metal gauntlets, "my patience wears exceedingly thin. Show me how to maximize the sphere's power."

He reached into a pocket in his cloak and pulled out a blood-red sphere. He caressed the sphere. It glowed, and Septimus' face contorted in pain.

"Figure it out for yourself," Septimus spat, struggling to breathe.

"Don't bother resisting," said Galderon, a cruel grin exposing his vampire-like teeth. He touched his sphere again, and Septimus screamed.

"Even if I knew how to help you, I wouldn't," Septimus said.

"Fool!" Galderon roared, slapping Septimus hard across the face with the back of his hand. "The other sphere has powers this one lacks—you built them both, you know how to fix mine. Make it work like it used to."

Galderon's sphere pulsated, the blood-red light growing ever brighter.

"Wait," he said. "It's the telepath. She's helping the children use their sphere again."

Kilaya snatched the sphere. She was breathing heavily and looked very scared. "That was too close," she said, regaining her composure. "He could have found out where we are."

"So Septimus *is* alive," said Eric. "My dream was right."

"We'd better tell Alcamarus."

CHAPTER TWELVE

SURVIVORS

DAWN was breaking when Eric, Jessica and Kilaya stepped out of the cave. The ocean was nowhere in sight.

"Find Zaliya. She'll get you something to eat. I need to talk to Alcamarus." Kilaya wandered off.

Zaliya was waiting for Eric and Jessica beside the dying ashes of a campfire.

"Here, have some breakfast." She handed Eric and Jessica pieces of bread and strips of dried meat. "You'll need to be strong for the journey ahead."

One of her wings was badly torn.

"Are you hurt?" asked Eric, gesturing to her wing.

"I'll be fine. A scaran attacked me, and I was lucky to get away. It'll get better soon. Alcamarus is a very skilled healer. But I won't be able to fly for a while."

"How many of us got away?" Jessica asked.

"Not many. We lost a lot of warriors." Zaliya sighed.

"We saw Karonvar fight the terexians," Eric said.

"Yes," said Zaliya sadly. "He knew he didn't have a chance against two of them. He gave his life to save you and the others."

"Did Tobias get away?" Jessica asked.

"I'm not sure. He may not have survived."

Eric and Jessica fell silent.

"Are we safe here?" Jessica asked.

"I hope so," replied Zaliya. "My people are from the plains of Tilatt, close to these mountains. They lived down there in the valley, until the scarans came. There were thousands of unicorns and griffins around here back then. Soon there'll be nothing left but the monsters that Galderon unleashed."

Alcamarus and Kilaya came over to join them. Alcamarus had a thick bandage on his left arm. His face was badly bruised.

"Kilaya told me what you saw," he began. "We need to rescue Septimus before Galderon forces him to tell everything he knows. It's vital that we get to the Citadel quickly. Let's get moving."

Alcamarus and Soldor had selected twenty of the best remaining warriors for the mission, along with Zaliya and Kilaya. They followed the bank of a river at the base of the Ligordian Mountains. Trees that looked like pine and spruce dominated the landscape. Late in the afternoon, ones resembling oak, maple, beech and elm became more common. Some cat-like creatures, with long, black bushy tails, rattled the branches above.

"What are those things called?" asked Eric.

"We call them leepers," said Zaliya.

"They look like cats, but they act like monkeys," said Eric, chuckling. He watched them jump from tree to tree.

"Look at that pig!" said Jessica, pointing to a furry creature in the water. It looked like a pig-headed beaver.

"That's a morvin. You don't see those very often. They hide in the underbrush."

Fascinated by the strange creatures around him, Eric almost forgot about the grim task that lay ahead.

THE group stopped to make camp in a small clearing. Alcamarus took Eric aside, and Jessica went with Soldor.

"I don't suppose you've ever fought with a sword before?" Alcamarus asked, as they reached an open space at the edge of the camp. Both moons were full.

"I took fencing lessons after school," Eric said. "Mom said it would be good exercise."

"So you know the basics," said Alcamarus. He handed Eric a long sword with a black hilt. "Feel the heft of the weapon."

Eric grabbed the cold handle and raised the sword, moving it from side to side.

"Good. Now I want you to watch me."

He demonstrated some simple moves, blocks and sword thrusts.

He makes it look so easy.

Then he handed Eric a shield and helped him

strap it to his arm. "All right. Let's see how you do against an opponent. I'm going to come at you, and you have to stop me and drive me back."

He took a few steps backward and drew his sword. "Let's go."

Alcamarus advanced and swung his sword. Eric blocked it with his shield. Alcamarus swung his sword again, from the other side. This time Eric blocked it with his own sword. The clang echoed through the valley. When Alcamarus thrust at Eric's midriff, Eric dodged and countered with a high blow of his own.

"Good," said Alcamarus, parrying with a sweep of his sword. "You've done well, but Galderon's warriors won't be quite so easy to fight. Let's go again."

After just over an hour, Alcamarus extended his hand to Eric. "Not bad for a beginner. Keep the sword. We'll start again in the morning."

Soldor came over with Jessica, who was carrying a short bow. She had a leather strap across her chest and a quiver filled with arrows on her back.

"She knows what she's doing," Soldor said.

"But there's still work to do."

"Until tomorrow," said Alcamarus. "We'll do more weapons training then, and Kilaya will help you master the sphere."

"We need to clean up a little," said Jessica. "Let's go down to the river."

When they reached the water, Eric and Jessica laid down their weapons beside a tree, and washed their hands and faces in the cool water. It was peaceful in the forest glade. The bright light of the moons shone through the canopy.

Something rustled in the bushes. Startled, Eric reached for his sword.

A small furry creature poked its head out of the shrubs. It looked like a cross between a rabbit and a raccoon, with long upright ears, grey fur and striped tail. Eric and Jessica watched as the fluffy little animal wandered to the edge of the water and drank. Then its ears perked up and it dashed into a hole by the base of a tree.

A branch cracked nearby. Suddenly a ten-foot terrorbird burst out of the bushes. It let out an ear-splitting screech, its crested head feathers spread wide in an attack posture.

"Grab the bow!" Eric yelled.

The terrorbird turned its attention to Eric, and charged. Eric dodged and slashed the monster's upper leg, infuriating it. With a screech, it swiped Eric with its forearm, knocking him to the ground. Eric thrust his sword up into the beast's belly, but it had no effect. Eric tried to scramble away, but the terrorbird grabbed his leg. Then suddenly it collapsed into the water, an arrow embedded in its neck.

"Thanks," Eric said as Jessica helped him up. "It looks pretty dead."

"I guess being the school archery champion paid off."

Eric was about to reply when Soldor and Alcamarus came hurrying down the path through the trees.

"I heard a terrorbird screech," said Alcamarus. "Are you all right?"

Soldor walked up to the bird. "It's not breathing," he said, pulling a long-bladed knife out from his sheath. "Now we have something for dinner."

CHAPTER THIRTEEN

THE POWER OF THE SPHERE

ERIC was surprised how good fire-roasted terrorbird tasted.

"We'll smoke the rest of it," Kilaya said, "and take it with us. Smoked terrorbird can last for months."

THE Brotherhood kept to the riverbank for a week, until they came to a thick tropical rainforest. Using Alcamarus' map, they avoided villages and other small settlements as they headed west. They kept a lookout for scarans, walking on paths hidden by trees to avoid being seen. They weren't attacked by any more terrorbirds, but one afternoon they had to take a long detour to avoid a roaming band of hungry terexians.

Every morning, before breakfast, Alcamarus

and Soldor gave Eric and Jessica training on how to use their swords and how to bow properly.

"You're both making good progress," Alcamarus said after a particularly robust workout.

"You're turning into genuine warriors," Soldor added.

"Still not much use against a malkonor," Jessica said.

Eric shivered, thinking back to that terrible day in Garoda.

Each evening, Kilaya helped Eric and Jessica with the sphere. They only trained for short periods, so that Galderon didn't have the chance to find them again.

"Why don't you use the sphere to enhance your telepathy?" Jessica asked Kilaya before one of their sessions. "Doesn't it like you?"

"Maybe because this sphere was created on Earth," Kilaya said, "only someone born there can push it to its full potential. That's probably why Septimus couldn't go through the portal on his own. Septimus made Galderon's sphere here in Koronada, so it should have given him ultimate power. I'm not sure why it hasn't."

"What do you mean by ultimate power?" asked Eric.

"It's just that. Power over everything—everything in our world, everything in your world, everything in any world that has ever been or could ever be."

"Even alternate realities or parallel universes?" asked Jessica.

"Yes. With this sphere, Galderon thinks he'll be able to shape reality any way he wishes. That's why he wants our sphere. He knows this one is more powerful."

"So, he could become a god," said Jessica.

"Yes, but he's not one yet," said Kilaya. "Galderon might not be able to handle being connected to everything in and out of existence. He's still only mortal."

"And the spheres only work with people that they like," said Eric. "Surely ours won't work with him."

"Maybe you're right," Kilaya said, "but there's no guarantee. Galderon probably thinks he can use his sphere to control ours, and force it to work for him. One thing I do know is that this rescue mission will be very dangerous—and we think you're the key to success, Eric."

"Me? Why?"

"You're from Earth, but have Koronada blood—this sphere was made on Earth with Koronada magic. That's why you're connected. Galderon was able to use his sphere to become powerful. You'll become powerful with this one."

"But I'm just a kid," said Eric. "I don't have any powers."

Kilaya handed Eric the sphere. "It enhances the powers you have, even if you don't know what they are. Now concentrate, Eric. Let your senses become one with the sphere. It might be overwhelming at first, but I'm sure you'll be able to master it."

Eric held it in his palm. He didn't hear the friendly voice this time, but the instant the sphere began glowing, he felt peaceful. Then his mind was flooded with hundreds of images and voices, all speaking at once. There was a little girl on a tire swing, and an older girl polishing an antique car. Only when he recognized Middle Wogglehole did Eric realize they were Jessica's memories.

"Eric," said Jessica, "I just saw you with your father, as a little boy."

"The sphere wants you to help me," Eric said. He wasn't sure why, but he knew it. "Here, put your hand on it."

"Focus," said Kilaya. "You're working together now. Your minds are one."

Eric concentrated, and Jessica did too. The sphere glowed even brighter.

Kilaya pointed to the campfire. "Now Eric, concentrate on the fire. Make the flames float."

The flames rose in the air until they were suspended above the glowing coals. Then they suddenly shot out across the clearing, singeing a low-hanging tree branch.

"Not bad," said Kilaya. "You just need to be able to direct it. We'll keep practising."

JESSICA was able to raise the flames herself, but, in the beginning, couldn't direct them. Over the following days, however, she and Eric improved steadily. It was clear that the sphere liked the two of them.

Kilaya taught them both how to use the sphere to harness the power of the elements. Jessica and Eric were able to summon small whirlwinds and freeze water. They learned how to conjure up small force fields that could serve as temporary shields. They had to be careful each time not to keep the sphere active for too long, in case Galderon detected it.

Soon they were ready to learn how to harness the power of lightning. Eric felt a tingling sensation in his fingertips, as static electricity crackled between his fingers.

"That's it, Eric," said Kilaya. "Now direct it at that tree. Focus. Concentrate."

Eric pointed at the tree, but the lightning almost hit Jessica. Luckily she conjured up a shield in time.

Kilaya clapped. "Well done, Jessica. Now you try."

Sparks jumped between her fingers, and she fired a blast of lightning.

Eric barely had time to create a shield and was

sent reeling along the forest floor.

He quickly got to his feet. "Are you trying to kill me?"

"I'm so sorry! I couldn't control it."

"You'll need to be quicker than that with a shield, Eric," Kilaya said with a frown. "That's all for now. You'll become experts at this soon enough. Let's get dinner."

Munching on a slice of smoked terrorbird, Jessica said, "I wonder if we'll ever really be good enough to defeat Galderon?"

"I know," said Kilaya. "I can sense your fears. But you have the inner strength to succeed."

"What makes you say that?"

"I'm a telepath. I'm always connected to the thoughts of others. There used to be many of us living in Kadosch before the war. I used to be able to connect with my fellow telepaths, but haven't sensed any of them for a long time. I may be the only one left alive."

THE Brotherhood finally arrived at the coast just south of the abandoned city of Villas, where the

Talonn River flowed down a waterfall into the sea. In the distance, across the straits, was the province of Tekara. Galderon's Citadel was on the far side of the province, on the western shore.

It was pouring rain as they arrived. Everyone was forced to take shelter in a large cave. When the rain finally stopped, Eric helped set up the camp, then wandered off to explore. A light mist filled the air. The forest was quiet and peaceful. Eric sat on a rock beside a small pond and watched the mist rise from the water. He gasped when he saw a hideous sabre-toothed creature hanging from a tree right above his head, snoring.

Scarans. There were lots of them, hanging upside down from their two thick leathery tails. They were dark-grey, scaly creatures, almost as large as terrorbirds. Their leathery wings were folded over their bodies, and their hands had deadly claws.

Eric was about to shout a warning to the others, but someone clasped a hand across his mouth from behind. It was Soldor. "Stay quiet. You don't want to wake them."

CHAPTER FOURTEEN

THE PERILOUS PATH

"SCARANS," Soldor told the others. "Hanging upside down from the trees."

"They're most likely the scarans that patrol the straits," said Zaliya. "They must be in hibernation. That's how they regenerate."

"So they're not dangerous right now?" said Eric.

"No," Zaliya replied, "but they will be if they're allowed to wake up. They never fly at night and are at their most vulnerable at dusk."

"How many are there?" Zaliya asked.

"About twenty, thirty," Soldor replied. "We should be able to handle them. But we can't risk any of them getting back to Galderon. We need a very strong barrier around where they're sleeping. As soon as one is killed, the others will know."

"We'll need a force field," Alcamarus said. "Eric and Jessica, you can do that."

"I'll help," Kilaya said. "We'll need maximum power to maintain a force field for that long."

"Let's get started," said Alcamarus, unsheathing his sword.

WHEN they reached the pond, Alcamarus, Soldor and the other warriors got into position, and Kilaya, Jessica and Eric stayed a few paces behind.

Soldor signalled that the warriors were ready, and Kilaya took out the sphere.

"Take my hands," said Kilaya. "Concentrate on erecting the force field. Don't lose it. Try to link our minds."

The sphere floated into the air, glowing. At first, Eric was flooded with memories from Jessica and Kilaya, but soon his mind was free to concentrate on the force field. The air began to shimmer and hum as the force field took shape.

"Close your eyes, Eric," Kilaya whispered. "You too, Jessica. You won't want to watch this."

Eric went into a dream-like state. Snow-capped

peaks, waterfalls and emerald meadows filled his mind, and he felt at peace. He was scarcely even aware of the passage of time. Then without warning, the visions were shattered by a high-pitched shriek. He opened his eyes to a scene of utter chaos.

Carcasses were scattered around. One scaran was still alive. Its wings were damaged, but it was still thrashing around, screeching and lashing out with its claws at the warriors. The force field was gone. Kilaya lay still, face down on the ground on the opposite side of the clearing. Jessica was nowhere to be seen. The wounded scaran stumbled then sprang at Eric, pinning him against a tree. It spat and snarled at him. The creature's red eyes burned with rage, and its deadly jaws were only inches from Eric's face.

Suddenly the scaran collapsed at Eric's feet. Soldor had impaled it with his sword.

"Are you okay, Eric?" Soldor asked.

"Yes, I think so," said Eric, shaking. "But where's Jessica? What happened?"

Soldor pointed to the other side of the pond.

Alcamarus and Jessica were helping Kilaya up.

"That was close," he said. "If this one had got away, Galderon would know where we are."

Zaliya led Eric and Jessica back to the camp as the last daylight faded away. She lit the campfire and they all warmed themselves around it.

"Close call back there," Eric said. "Good thing Soldor got that scaran. I didn't even see it until it was too late. I was really lucky."

"You two try and get some rest," said Zaliya. "We have an early start in the morning."

Zaliya went back to the pond, and Eric and Jessica settled in beside the fire.

"Are you sure you're okay?" Eric asked Jessica. "You still look a bit nervous."

"I'm all right," she replied. But then added, "Well, not really. I keep thinking about the village. We're a long way from Middle Wogglehole, Eric. I can't help wondering if we'll ever go back to Earth."

"I hope we do," Eric said. "That was really scary with the scaran, and there could be worse to come."

"I honestly don't know how much more of this I can take."

"No one said this was going to be easy. It's up to us. We have to save Septimus. Let's get to sleep. You'll feel better in the morning."

But Eric couldn't sleep. He watched the dancing flames and thought about the tiny fire figure back at Ivy Cottage. It seemed so long ago now.

"WAKE up, Eric," Zaliya said. "It's time. We need to go to the cliffs."

Eric sat up and rubbed his eyes. It was still dark but there was a faint light on the horizon. Zaliya nudged Jessica, who was on the opposite side of the fire.

Zaliya led Eric and Jessica up to the top of the cliff. Kilaya was waiting there with Alcamarus, Soldor and the rest of the warriors. Dawn broke over the western horizon, and the coast of Tekara slowly came into view. At Alcamarus' feet lay the wings of the dead scarans.

"With no scarans patrolling," Zaliya pointed out, "we'll be able to fly across the straits."

"Fly?" said Eric.

"Yes, fly," Alcamarus replied. "The olokarens are everywhere down there. It's safer in the air than in the sea."

Zaliya held up a pair of scaran wings. "We've cut slits into the wings so that you can slip your arms inside them," she told him. "We'll tie some branches to them to keep them outstretched."

"Zaliya will take you up high and drop you," said Kilaya. "You'll glide over to the beach on the other side."

"But Zaliya, what about your wing?" Eric said.

"I'm much better now, Eric. I'll take Soldor and the warriors up first so they can secure the beach. They'll go one at a time, but I can lift both of you at once. Kilaya, Alcamarus and I will be the last ones to leave."

Once Soldor and the rest of the warriors had slipped into the scaran wings, Zaliya began carrying them aloft. She struggled to lift Soldor, but managed to fly far enough above the strait before letting him go. Soldor glided out of sight, and, after hovering for a few moments, Zaliya returned. "He was heavier than I expected. But he made it safely to the beach."

She took the warriors up one by one, and they glided out of sight toward Tekara.

"Remember your weapons," said Alcamarus. He handed Eric his sword and Jessica her bow and arrows. "Be ready to use them. You never know."

Eric sheathed his sword, and Jessica slung her quiver over her shoulder. She pulled on her scaran wings, looking apprehensive. Alcamarus handed Eric his wings and he slipped them on. The leathery wings were thin and surprisingly light, but felt cold and clammy against his skin. Eric shuddered as he slid his arms into them. His stomach churned, and he took a few deep breaths.

This is disgusting.

"Keep your arms spread out wide," Zaliya said. "The air currents will carry you all the way over."

"You need to get off the beach as soon as you land," added Kilaya. "Take off your wings right away or they'll slow you down."

"Ready?" said Zaliya

Eric swallowed hard. Zaliya grabbed them

around the waist, unfurled her wings and flew up high. A lush green forest spread out along the coastline on the opposite side of the strait.

Zaliya let go of Eric first, and he fought to steady himself in the wind. Flying high above the waves was exhilarating. It was like nothing Eric had ever experienced, and a feeling of elation swept over him.

Eric stumbled when he hit the sand. Then he slipped out of the wings and let them fall to the ground. Jessica was right behind him, but landed knee-deep in the water. She took off her wings and let them float away.

Scanning the beach, Eric couldn't see any signs of Soldor and the warriors. *They must be hiding in the trees*, he thought.

He turned to Jessica. Two tentacles rose from the water behind her.

"Jessica!" Eric shouted. "Olokarens! Run!"

Jessica screamed as a tentacle wrapped around her chest and pulled her into the water. Eric drew his sword and raced into the waves. He slashed repeatedly at the olokaren's twisting tentacles, and severed two of them. The olokaren shrieked and raised two other tentacles. It kept its grip on Jessica and pulled her into the surf. Dodging the snapping tentacles, Eric swung his sword and cut off one of the creature's eyestalks. Then he thrust his sword into its head. The olokaren screeched in pain and slumped into the water.

Soldor and the warriors came rushing out from the forest. Jessica jumped up and loaded her bow.

"Leave it!" Eric yelled as the wounded olokaren retreated into the waves.

"Eric! Jessica!" Soldor called out. "Are you all right?"

"Yeah," said Eric. "Jessica? Are you okay?"

"I'm fine, I think," Jessica replied. Blood trickled from a bite mark on her forehead.

Soldor looked out over the waves and into the woods beside the beach, his sword drawn. Alcamarus and Kilaya glided onto the sand, closely followed by Zaliya.

"We saw it all from the sky," said Alcamarus as he took off his wings, "but there was nothing we could do."

"There will be more of them," said Soldor urgently. "The sun's almost up."

They hurried from the beach so that Alcamarus could tend to Jessica's wounds in the safety of the forest. Standing at the edge of the trees, Eric took a long look at the straits. He shuddered at the thought of all the other dangers they were likely to face in Galderon's realm.

A branch cracked, and Eric froze. Something moved. *A terrorbird?* he thought. He gripped his sword. *Or a scaran? A terexian?* But a familiar figure staggered onto the beach.

"Tobias!"

CHAPTER FIFTEEN

INTO THE CITADEL

ERIC raced over to Tobias, who'd fallen to his knees on the sand. He had a deep bloody gash on his arm that ran all the way down from his shoulder.

"Eric," Tobias gasped. "You are alive! Is Jessica all right?"

"She's fine," Eric replied, "but what about you? What happened to your arm?"

"A malkonor slashed me," said Tobias. He was holding the matted hair on his arm. "The bleeding has slowed, but I need medical attention."

"Alcamarus is just over there," Eric said. "He'll be able to help you."

"JESSICA'S wounds were minor," Alcamarus said as he cleaned the gash on Tobias' arm. "Tobias, what happened to you?"

"It was back in the Forest of Orbann, when we were attacked by Galderon's army," Tobias began. "I ended up in a fight with a malkonor who gave me this wound. When he blasted me with fire, I was sure that I was dead. Instead I woke up at the Citadel."

"That's where Septimus is!" said Eric.

"Did you see him?" asked Jessica. "Is he all right?"

"He is alive," said Tobias, "but barely."

"How did you escape?" asked Eric.

"Galderon is getting careless. He was so focused on getting Septimus to tell him how to make his sphere work to its full capacity, he did not watch me closely. I slipped out through one of the tunnels used by the scarans. Once I was out of the Citadel, I made my way to the coast. I have been hiding here, wondering how long it would be before Galderon found me."

"Hard to believe the former Lord Protector of Tekara was so lucky," said Soldor, narrowing his eyes.

Alcamarus put a hand on Soldor's shoulder.

"That's enough of that," he said. "Tobias is back now. He can help us plan our attack on the Citadel."

"I would be honoured to serve you," said Tobias.

"Maybe we could use the scaran tunnels to get inside," Kilaya said.

"Yes, they are only used by the scarans, so they are not very well guarded," said Tobias. "The time to enter is when the scarans are asleep. The tunnels will be empty then."

"How far is the Citadel from here?" asked Eric.

"Not very far," replied Tobias. "Just a little way through the Aktalian Forest. From there we just have to cross the Oksus River."

"We could be there before nightfall," Alcamarus said.

"The malkonors and the other creatures are all on the other side of the straits, looking for you," said Tobias. "There are guards at the Citadel, but I know how to avoid them. We need to hurry. Galderon will notice that I am not there, if he has not already."

"So," said Alcamarus, "let's move out quickly."

The Brotherhood trekked through the forest for the rest of the day without encountering any of Galderon's monsters. They crossed the Oksus River with little difficulty. It was early evening when they saw the Citadel at the top of the cliff. A vast whirlpool of dark clouds dominated the sky above the black towers and turrets. Lightning flashed everywhere.

The openings to the tunnels dotted the cliff face. Guards were posted along the walls of the Citadel, but Galderon's creatures were nowhere to be seen.

"You were right," said Soldor to Tobias, nodding. "There really aren't many guards."

"Galderon is overconfident," said Tobias. "He has no idea we are here."

"So how are we getting up to those tunnels?" Eric asked. "Is Zaliya flying us up there?"

"It's too dangerous," said Jessica. "The guards would see us."

"Yes, we will have to climb," Tobias replied. "But it is not practical for us all to use the tunnels."

"Agreed," said Alcamarus, nodding his head. "I'll lead the way. Kilaya, you follow, but stay close to Eric and Jessica; Tobias, you can bring up the rear. Once we get inside, we'll be able to surprise the guards and open the main gate for Soldor, Zaliya and the others."

"As you wish," Tobias said. "We leave at nightfall."

ONCE it was dark enough, Alcamarus led Eric, Jessica, Kilaya and Tobias to the base of the cliff. After securing their weapons, they began climbing. Eric slipped more than once, and Jessica lost her footing just as they reached the opening, but Tobias held her. It was very dark inside the tunnel. Eric held out the sphere and it glowed. He went first, lighting their way. The tunnel was wide, but the ceiling was low, and they had to stoop from time to time to avoid hitting their heads. No one spoke.

Suddenly there was an ominous rumble followed by a loud crash, and the ceiling of the tunnel collapsed just behind Jessica and Eric, leaving them alone.

"Alcamarus!" yelled Jessica. "Are you okay?"

There was no response.

"They're trapped!" Jessica exclaimed. "We have to help them!"

"There's nothing we can do!"

"But—"

"Look," Eric said. "I'm sure they're going back out the other way."

"But they could be hurt, or even dead," said Jessica. "How do you know they're even still alive?"

"I don't," Eric admitted, "but if they make it back to join Soldor and the others, we need to open the gates for them."

Eric pulled Jessica through the tunnel and into a narrow corridor inside the Citadel.

"How will we find the way without Tobias?"

Eric held out the sphere. "We can use this."

Jessica touched his hand. "No. Put it away. Galderon will find us if we use it for more than just a light. Even that might be risky."

"Right." Eric put the sphere back in his pocket and drew his sword. "Then let's hope we can find the way to the gate, before anyone notices we're here."

They crept along a corridor. Torches lined the walls at regular intervals. Eventually they clambered up a spiral staircase into a circular room surrounded by stone pillars. A stone archway stood in the centre. Septimus was slumped against one of the pillars, secured by chains.

Eric and Jessica rushed over to him. Septimus was pale, and his eyes were half-closed. He had cuts on his forehead, bruises on his sunken cheeks, and his thick hair was matted with blood.

"Dad! It's me, Eric. Are you okay?"

Septimus slowly raised his head. "Eric," he murmured. "Jessica?"

"How touching," said a deep voice behind them.

Eric and Jessica whirled around and saw a white-haired, bearded man wearing black armour, standing near the archway.

It was Galderon.

CHAPTER SIXTEEN

THE PRICE OF POWER

TWO of Galderon's guards stepped out from behind the pillars. They drew their swords and stood their ground a few feet in front of Eric and Jessica.

"I was so enjoying torturing him," said Galderon. His grim smile revealed his deadly vampire teeth. "He wouldn't tell me the secret of the sphere's power, despite all the pain he suffered."

Galderon caressed the red sphere in his hand.

"I know the sphere you have is more powerful," he continued, barely concealing a sneer. "I saw the telepath show you how to work it. And now you've brought me the sphere, so I have no further use for him. Give it to me."

The guards took a step forward. Eric brandished his sword and Jessica took out her bow. But

Galderon waved his hand, and the weapons were dragged from their grasps. Eric's sword shattered as if it were glass, and Jessica's bow was broken in two.

"Focus the lightning, Eric," shouted Jessica.

Eric took out the sphere and it began to glow. It floated up from his hand and hung in the air beside his head. The electricity crackled between their fingers.

"Don't be a fool, boy," snarled Galderon. His sphere also began to glow. "Hand it over."

Eric and Jessica quickly created shields just as Galderon shot lightning bolts at each of them. The lighting bounced off the shields, striking one guard in the chest and the other's outstretched sword. They both fell to the floor.

Eric and Jessica took refuge behind a pillar, but Galderon blasted it to pieces. They cowered in the rubble.

"Stop wasting my time," said Galderon. "Give me the sphere."

Eric slipped the sphere into his pocket and huddled next to Jessica behind a pile of stones.

"Let's split up," he whispered. "Galderon won't know which of us has the sphere. We should use the fire from the torches, too. Maybe we'll catch him off guard."

Jessica ran one way, darting from one pillar to the next as she evaded Galderon's blasts. Eric dashed the other way, conjuring shields for protection as he ran. Jessica pulled fire from the torches and aimed at Galderon as she edged over to the stone archway, but he simply brushed her blaze aside with a wave of his hand.

"Fire together!" Eric yelled.

Jessica nodded, and they attacked Galderon with a barrage of flames from both sides. He staggered under their joint onslaught, but still blocked every attack. Eric and Jessica were no match for him.

Galderon intensified his attacks and Jessica's shields weakened. Eric scrambled to help her, taking cover where he could, but before he reached her, Jessica's shield faltered under a massive blast of lightning.

"Jessica!"

She lay still, slumped against the wall.

Galderon fired at Eric. He created a shield; but the attack was too powerful, and Eric was slammed against a pillar. Eric slid to the floor and couldn't move his arms or legs. He watched helplessly as Galderon searched Jessica for the sphere. Galderon then approached Eric, reached down and pulled the blue sphere roughly from Eric's pocket. A vicious smile spread across Galderon's face as he slipped the red sphere into his pocket and held up the blue sphere in triumph.

Galderon walked back over to the archway, stood in front of the frame and opened his hand. The blue sphere floated upward, suspended in mid-air. The archway's portal opened, revealing gateways to countless worlds.

"Finally," he said. "Ultimate power!" Galderon held up his hand. "Stop," he ordered. But thousands of images continued to flash across the archway.

"Stop!" Galderon roared again, and still nothing. He angrily snatched at the floating sphere, but a bolt of lightning shot out and narrowly missed his head.

The sphere dropped to the floor and stopped glowing. Galderon approached it cautiously, but the sphere rolled toward Eric and came to a stop at his feet.

It began glowing again.

It's trying to tell me something. Eric glanced at Septimus, then at Jessica. Neither of them were moving. As the feeling came back to his arms and legs, Eric knew what he had to do. He scooped up the sphere and got to his feet. It began to glow brighter, and Eric once again felt the lightning crackle between his fingers.

"Fool!" Galderon roared. "You still resist?" He took out the red sphere, which glowed more intensely.

The blue sphere grew fainter in Eric's hand. *It's losing power!*

"So," snarled Galderon, "it seems your sphere doesn't work anymore. It appears that the girl was needed; you can't use it alone. Now that she's dead, my sphere is the most powerful."

He stepped forward and grabbed Eric firmly by the wrist, almost crushing the bones. Eric was forced onto his knees, and he dropped his sphere.

Galderon picked it up and slapped Eric hard across the face with the back of his hand, sending him sprawling over to where Jessica lay in the rubble.

"And now," said Galderon, holding both spheres in his hands, "everything that ever was, and ever will be, is mine."

Eric reached over and touched Jessica's neck, but couldn't find a pulse.

Galderon released the two spheres and they floated upward in front of the portal. The blue sphere's glow grew fainter as it orbited the blazing red one.

"Eric," Jessica whispered. Her eyes flickered to life.

"Jessica! You're alive!"

"I hope so," she murmured, sitting up. "What's Galderon doing?"

"He couldn't get our sphere to work," Eric replied. "It doesn't like him. But now he's using his sphere to control it."

"So it's all over," said Jessica. "He's won."

"Maybe not," whispered Eric. "We may still have a chance. Kilaya said that Galderon might not be able to handle the terrible power the two spheres will generate together."

Eric and Jessica slowly rose to their feet. Galderon had his back to them and didn't notice.

Images continued to shift steadily across the frame. Then there was a pause. In the archway, Eric could see the city of Garoda as it must have looked before the war. Galderon raised his hand and the city disappeared, replaced by views of millions of strange alien worlds.

"Yes!" declared Galderon, triumphantly. "I can feel it all—the memories and thoughts of each and every being in a billion, billion worlds—ultimate power!"

The images flashed across the frame at an incredible speed. The blue sphere spun faster and faster around the red one.

Suddenly Galderon dropped to his knees, hands pressed hard against his temples.

"What's happening?" he roared, his reptilian features twisted in agony.

"Quick, the spheres!" Eric shouted.

They dashed forward and Eric snatched the blue sphere, while Jessica grabbed the red one.

"Well, you wanted to control everything that is or ever will be," Eric declared.

Galderon screamed in pain, clutching his head.

"Throw his sphere through the arch!" Eric shouted to Jessica.

Jessica flung the red sphere into the portal. There was a massive explosion of light, and Galderon was gone. The blast flung Eric and Jessica against the wall. Within the arch, there was a swirling flash of colours and blurred shapes. Then a whirlwind swept around the circular room. Jessica clung to one of the chains binding Septimus to the pillar, and Eric grabbed her hand before he could be swept into the swirling vortex. He held tightly onto Septimus' sphere as dozens of guards from the rest of the Citadel were pulled into the whirlpool.

The wind grew even stronger. Eric watched in astonishment as hundreds of terexians, scarans, olokarens, terrorbirds and malkonors were all sucked into the Citadel through the open spaces between the pillars. The monsters swirled around the room before being swept through the archway.

Then as suddenly as it had appeared, the tornado was gone and the stone frame was empty.

"It's over," said Eric with relief, standing up.

"You had me worried there for a moment," Jessica said.

Eric cradled the blue sphere in his hand. It had stopped glowing.

Eric and Jessica unbuckled Septimus' chains, and eased him onto the stone floor.

"It's not over yet," said a voice behind them.

They both whirled around to see Kilaya, who was standing with Alcamarus and Tobias.

"You're alive!" exclaimed Jessica.

She rushed over to embrace them all, as did Eric.

"We saw what happened," said Tobias. "We were sheltering from the whirlwind over by the entrance to the spiral staircase."

"How did you escape the tunnel?" Eric asked.

"We were lucky," Tobias admitted. "I pulled Kilaya back just in time. When we realized our path was completely blocked, we climbed down the cliff and joined the others."

"They'd already taken care of Galderon's guards," added Kilaya. "Zaliya flew inside and opened the main gate."

Alcamarus examined Septimus. "His life force is almost depleted."

Septimus' face was devoid of colour, his eyes bloodshot. Alcamarus gently moved his hands down in front of Septimus' face, and his colour slowly returned. Septimus' injuries faded, leaving only a dark bruise on his cheek.

"Eric, Jessica," he gasped, "I'm so glad you're okay. It was as if I was watching it through someone else's eyes. I was powerless to help."

"I'm alright," Eric assured him. "Kilaya taught us well."

"She certainly must have," Septimus agreed, with a smile. "How on earth did you know how to defeat Galderon?"

"I didn't really know," Eric confessed. "It was a gamble to let him take the sphere. I figured that, once Galderon was linked to all the other dimensions, his mind would be overwhelmed. I had no idea about the tornado, though."

"I hope he's gone for good," said Jessica.

"Yes," Kilaya said. "He's probably stranded in any one of a trillion worlds, with no hope of return. The monsters were all linked to Galderon's mind too. That's how he controlled them, but that's what caused them to be brought here to share his fate."

"And now we can finally rebuild our world," said Alcamarus.

"We can help," said Eric.

"You have helped us enough," Tobias replied. "Thanks to you, I will soon see my beloved family again. I have learned that they survived and sought refuge in Garanbal." He turned to Septimus. "Will you stay with us here in Koronada?"

"No, I'm afraid not. Earth is my home," he said, putting an arm around Eric's shoulder and pulling him close.

"We must move quickly," said Kilaya. "The portal is very unstable."

"Eric, we need you to open the portal," said

Septimus. "We all need to work together and focus our thoughts on the village."

"Once you reach the other side," Kilaya said, "the portal here will be sealed. Without a sphere, we'll have no way of opening it. And we'll destroy the archway, just to be sure."

The sphere began glowing in Eric's hand. After quickly saying their farewells, Eric, Jessica and Septimus joined hands and stood in front of the archway. They all concentrated on Middle Wogglehole until they could see the ruined castle on the hilltop, then the church and finally Septimus' workshop.

"Now!" Septimus shouted. And without a backward glance, they stepped through the archway and vanished.

CHAPTER SEVENTEEN

FULL CIRCLE

SEPTIMUS, Jessica and Eric stumbled onto the path in front of the workshop at Ivy Cottage.

"We made it," Eric said, steadying himself. "It worked."

"Will you ever be able to go back?" said Jessica.

"No," Septimus said. "The portal's been sealed. But it's all for the best." He sighed. "I don't know about you two, but it seems like an eternity since I had something to eat. How about some lunch?"

They went into the kitchen, but there was nothing in the fridge, and the cabinets were empty.

"Well, it looks like I can't offer you any lunch," Septimus apologized. "At least not at the moment. Why don't you two head over to the shop and get some bread, milk and maybe some bacon and eggs?"

"Yoo hoo. Anyone home?"

Mrs. Pierce swept into the kitchen. She was wearing another colourful flower print dress and her hair looked as if she'd just stepped out of the salon. "Well hello there, everyone," she said with a broad smile.

"Marigold!" exclaimed Septimus, smiling back at her.

Eric and Jessica grinned at each other.

"I mean, Mrs. Pierce," Septimus said, blushing. "How are you?"

"I wasn't sure if anyone was home," she said, "since the motorbike was gone."

"Oh yes," Septimus said, "the motorbike, of course. It's—er—at the repair shop. Yes, that's it. Getting fixed up a little."

"Probably about time," said Mrs. Pierce, with a chuckle. "I sometimes think that motorbike's as old as you are. And what on earth are you all wearing?"

All three of them still wore clothes from Koronada, dirty and stained with blood.

"These?" said Eric, thinking quickly. "We've

been helping out in the workshop."

"And what on earth have you done to your face, Septimus?" asked Mrs. Pierce, concerned. "Where did you get that massive bruise?"

"Oh, this," Septimus began, touching his cheek. "Oh, I—er . . ."

"He banged his head on a cupboard door in the workshop," Jessica explained.

"Yes, yes," said Septimus, "that's right, in the workshop . . . absolutely."

"You and your workshop," remarked Mrs. Pierce, with a grin. "Well, it certainly looks painful. Shall I get started on watering the flowers and plants then?"

"Perhaps later," Septimus replied. "We were just going out. I need to check on the progress with the motorbike and the children were about to pick up some groceries. I seem to be out of just about everything."

"Honestly," said Mrs. Pierce, with a wry smile, as she gently elbowed Septimus in the ribs. "I sometimes wonder how he copes at all. He never even leaves our little village. Anyway, I'd better go and open the shop for you if you need those groceries. See you later."

"You aren't actually going to the repair shop, of course," said Eric, once Mrs. Pierce had gone.

"No," Septimus replied with a chuckle, "but we really do need those groceries."

When they stepped outside, Eric looked up at the castle. The storm clouds had disappeared and the sun was shining brightly. *It really is all over.*

"Right, I'll see you two later," said Septimus, before heading into his workshop.

"Come on, Eric," said Jessica. "I'm starving."

They waved to Septimus and hurried off along the narrow lane that led to the village.